Race Further with Reading

The FANTASY Football Wall

By Ann Bryant

Illustrated by Kelly Kennedy

W
FRANKLIN WATTS
LONDON•SYDNEY

CHAPTER 1
The Match

Harry got changed at top speed for the football match.

"Do you think we'll win, Mr Gates?" he asked his teacher.

A boy called Brad answered first.

"No, Yardley school have got better players than our Berry school team."

Harry went red. He knew he wasn't as good at football as Brad.

"Just do your best. That's what matters," said Mr Gates. "Come on everyone," he added, "time to warm up!"

Off they jogged to the football pitch, chanting, "Berry School is the best!" No one chanted louder than Harry. He so wanted his team to win.

By half-time the score was one-nil
to Yardley.

"Keep it up everyone. We've still got
a good chance," said Mr Gates.

In the second half Harry tried harder
than ever. As soon as he spotted Brad in
a great position to score, he kicked the
ball perfectly to Brad's feet.

A second later, there was an enormous cheer as the ball shot straight from the tip of Brad's boot into the back of the net. "Goal! Yessss!"

It was a brilliant moment. Harry was hoping Brad might high-five him for helping make the goal. But he didn't.

For the next twenty minutes the ball flew up and down the pitch. Then came the moment when one of the Yardley players was about to score. Harry ran like the wind, determined to stop that goal. He got to the ball just in time to kick it out of the way.

"Well done, Harry!" cried Mr Gates.

Then there followed a huge groan from the whole Berry team. Harry's kick had sent the ball off the pitch.

"Corner kick to Yardley," called Mr Gates.

"What did you do that for?" Brad hissed at Harry.

Harry didn't have time to answer before a
massive cheer went up. The Yardley team
had scored from the corner kick. Then the
whistle blew. The match was over and once
again Yardley had won.

"Great effort, everyone!" said Mr Gates,
as the team went back to the changing
room. "You couldn't have played better."
"Apart from Harry," muttered Brad. "It was
his fault we lost."

Mr Gates didn't hear that. But Harry did.
And his spirits sank down to his boots.

CHAPTER 2
No Ordinary Wall

It was break time and Harry was playing football in the playground. But he wasn't concentrating. He was looking over at a very steep hill on the other side of the playground. It was called the Mound and no one was allowed near it. Harry liked pretending that a monster lived inside it.

He snapped out of his daydream to find the ball flying towards him.

"Get it, Harry!" called Brad. "You're the nearest!" Harry ran after the ball as it rolled onto the playground. Then he kicked it by mistake. By the time he caught up with it, he was right beside the Mound.

"Harry Bing!" called Mrs Carter, the dinner lady, crossly. "Come away from the Mound this instant! You know it is forbidden to play there. Now go and stand by the wall for three minutes!"

Children had to stand by the wall if they were naughty. Harry trudged off to stand by the wall for three minutes.

He was sure Brad had kicked the ball hard on purpose to get him into trouble. Ever since the match against Yardley, Brad had been mean to him.

He sighed and stared at the wall. Maybe if he invented a game it would make the three minutes go faster.

Yes, he could pretend the wall was a massive computer with super powers. He was controlling the computer...

...and every brick in the wall was someone in the school.

"Okay, this one is Brad Bates," he whispered, touching the brick right in front of his nose. "Make him fall over."

At that very moment a screech filled the air.

Harry looked across at the football game.

Brad was on the ground. He got up a

moment later with a scowl on his face and

said, "Someone tripped me."

Harry's eyes flew open and his heart

beat faster. Did the wall really have

super powers?

No, that was impossible. All the same he would try it again. Tapping the brick that glowed, he said, "Make Mrs Carter blow her whistle."

No sooner had Harry finished speaking than Mrs Carter blew her whistle. Immediately everyone stood still. "Time to line up!" she announced.

But Harry didn't want to line up. He wanted to stay at the wall. It really did have super powers. It was totally brilliant. He quickly tapped the glowing brick again. "Make Mrs Lee forget all about that test she said she was going to give us this afternoon."

When the bell rang Harry got ready very slowly. Then he went to the library and spent ages choosing a book. Finally, when everyone else had gone home, he slipped into the empty playground and hurried over to the wall. His heart was thudding with excitement. This was going to be great fun.

"Right," he said out loud, "I think I'll start with the school cook." Harry reached up and tapped the glowing brick.

"Make Mrs Blanch put chocolate mousse on the menu every day this term!"

Then there came a sudden noise like a growl from behind the wall. He gasped. The growling grew louder. Maybe a monster really did live in the Mound. It was just behind the wall. Harry's heart thumped as a wisp of smoke curled out of the top.

Was the monster a dragon? He nearly jumped out of his skin at the sound of footsteps right behind him.

"Who were you talking to?"

It was a shock to see Brad standing there.

"No one."

"Yes you were. And you were tapping the wall. I saw you."

Harry was so filled with fear he could hardly speak. "There's a dragon..." was all he managed to utter.

"That's a bulldozer you can hear. It's on the other side of the wall," said Brad, sneering. "They're flattening the Mound to make more playground. Didn't you even know that?"

"But what about...the dragon?"

"Don't talk rubbish!" said Brad.

"There's no such thing as dragons."

He turned to walk away, but turned back almost immediately as a sharp shriek filled the air. Then both boys stared in horror as the top of the Mound erupted to reveal an angry green and silver dragon.

CHAPTER 4
Stop the Bulldozer!

The dragon spread its spiky leather wings and arched its neck. With one leap, it launched itself into the playground, its gleaming eyes fixed on Harry and Brad.

Then with a shuddering breath, it suddenly stopped next to the Mound.

Brad trembled and clutched hold of Harry. "Quick!" he hissed urgently. "It's falling asleep! Let's go before it wakes up."

He'd only taken a few steps when there
came an angry roar. The dragon had
woken and reared up, nostrils flared. Brad
shot straight back to Harry's side and stood
there, shaking. Then, letting out a long
snort, the dragon flopped down once again.

"We're trapped," whispered Brad.

"Maybe not," said Harry, a thoughtful look on his face.

"What do you mean?" asked Brad, grabbing Harry's arm.

"The wall has super powers," said Harry.

"We just need to find the glowing brick."

Brad looked as though he was about to
sneer, but then changed his mind.

"So m...make the bulldozer g...get to work!"
he stammered. But the words were no
sooner out of his mouth than something
incredible happened. Two tiny dragons
slowly clambered out of the Mound.

One of them tumbled down it and rolled close to the sleeping dragon. The other one fell back inside.

"The mother dragon is protecting her babies," breathed Harry. "She thought we were going to harm them."

And at that very moment a gravelly grating roar filled the air. The bulldozers were at work, and the mother dragon hadn't even stirred from her deep sleep. "We've got to warn her!" said Harry. "The baby dragon in the Mound will get completely crushed."

Brad seemed frozen to the spot. "W...what can we d...do?"

"We must stop the bulldozers," said Harry.

"But how?" asked Brad, his teeth chattering with fear.

"Tap every single brick in the wall," said Harry firmly, "until we find the right one. With each tap, say the words: Make the bulldozers stop!"

Brad's face was white with worry.

"Go!" said Harry.

The boys worked and worked, jumping for the high bricks, reaching for the far away bricks, bending for the low ones. Together they tapped and tapped until suddenly the noise of the bulldozers stopped.

"We've done it!" cried Brad.

Harry gulped. "We still have to warn the mother dragon," he said.

"No way," said Brad, wide-eyed.

Harry didn't reply. Taking a deep breath he crept towards the dragon on shaky legs. He'd never felt more scared in his life as he reached out and touched her wrinkled neck.

Instantly she raised her head. Harry pointed to the baby dragon next to her. The dragon's eyes flashed and she picked it up in her mouth. Then with a flick of her tail she scooped the other baby out of the Mound. A moment later she had taken off into the sky.

Harry and Brad were glued to the spot. They watched in amazement as the dragon rose over the playground with her babies. Over the woods she soared. Up and away she flew, until she was no more than a tiny dot in the distance.

CHAPTER 5
The Rematch

The next day Harry got to school early.
He went into the playground to find Brad
waiting for him. Brad looked wide-eyed.
"Did it really happen, Harry?" he asked.
Harry nodded. "I think so. Let's test it again."
He found the glowing brick and tapped it.
"Make us beat Yardley this afternoon."

The Berry vs Yardley match was the most exciting game ever. With less than a minute to go the score was one-nil to Berry. But the Yardley team had the ball.

"Go Harry!" screamed Brad, as a Yardley player booted the ball towards the goal.

It was happening exactly the same as in the last match. Harry ran his hardest and managed to kick the ball out of the way just in time.

But this time Brad was in position. He stopped the ball going off the pitch and dribbled it back up the field.

"Great team work!" yelled Mr Carter,

as the final whistle blew.

The match was over. Berry had won.

Harry and Brad went to pick up their sweaters from behind the goal. It was then that they saw it – a tiny hard green egg, covered in silver swirls.

"Wow!" gasped Brad.

"Let's take it to the woods," whispered Harry. "It'll be safe there."

44

So, when no one was looking they slipped off and gently placed the egg in a hollow tree trunk.

Jogging back onto the field they heard a swishing sound from high above and they both looked up. Two bright eyes glinted down at them from the blue sky. Then one of them closed and opened again.

A moment later the sky clouded over.

"Come on you two heroes!" called Mr Carter from the other end of the field. "You did brilliantly today, you know!"

Brad grinned at Harry. Harry grinned back. And the two of them high-fived each other.

"Yes, we did!"

First published in 2014 by
Franklin Watts
338 Euston Road
London
NW1 3BH

Franklin Watts Australia
Level 17/207 Kent Street
Sydney
NSW 2000

Text © Ann Bryant 2014
Illustration © Kelly Kennedy 2014

The rights of Ann Bryant to be
identified as the author and Kelly Kennedy
as the illustrator of this Work have been
asserted in accordance with the Copyright,
Designs and Patents Act, 1988.

Series Editor: Melanie Palmer
Series Advisor: Catherine Glavina
Series Designer: Cathryn Gilbert

A CIP catalogue record for this book is
available from the British Library.

ISBN 978 1 4451 3365 2 (hbk)
ISBN 978 1 4451 3366 9 (pbk)
ISBN 978 1 4451 3368 3 (ebook)
ISBN 978 1 4451 3367 6 (library ebook)

Printed in China

Franklin Watts is a division of Hachette
Children's Books, an Hachette UK company.
www.hachette.co.uk